PINGU

the Chef

BBC CHILDREN'S BOOKS

Pingu's mum and dad were going off for the day to visit some friends.

"Bye-bye Pingu and Pinga. Be good while we're away," called Mum and Dad as they drove off in the post truck.

2

As soon as Mum and Dad were out of sight, Pingu and Pinga rushed indoors to have some fun.

"Let's make some popcorn," said Pinga.

"Good idea," said Pingu.

Pinga found the corn while Pingu got the pan ready on the stove.

Ding, ding, ding! The corn bounced into the saucepan.

As it cooked the corn burst open – pop, pop, pop!

Pingu and Pinga munched away until there were only three pieces left.

"Those are mine," said Pingu to Pinga.
"You've had more than me."

"Oooh!" said Pinga. "Look at that hole in the ceiling."

As Pingu looked up, Pinga was finishing off the last pieces of popcorn. Pingu was furious.

"There's only one thing for it," said Pingu. "We'll just have to make some more."

He opened the store cupboard and came face to face with more corn than he'd ever seen in his life.

"Wow!" gasped Pingu.

It took Pingu a very long time to get all the corn ready. The pieces came off one by one and pinged into the box.

When every bit of corn was in the box, Pingu carefully poured the whole lot into his mum's big stewing pot.

Pop, pop, pop! The corn began to cook. Suddenly the lid lifted off and out came a torrent of popcorn that chased Pingu and Pinga out of the room.

"What shall we do with it?"
gasped Pinga in horror. "We
can't eat all *that*!"

"We'll have to give it away,"
said Pingu.

10

Pinga shovelled corn into boxes as fast as she could, while Pingu loaded the boxes on to his sledge.

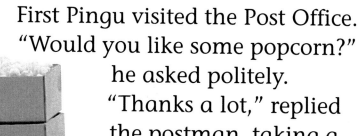

First Pingu visited the Post Office.
"Would you like some popcorn?"
he asked politely.
"Thanks a lot," replied
the postman, taking a
box from Pingu. "It's one
of my favourite things."

Next Pingu visited Mrs McGreedy.
"Would your baby penguins
like some popcorn?" he asked.
"I'm sure they would,"
said Mrs McGreedy.
"Come along in."

13

"Yippee! Popcorn!" cried Mrs McGreedy's babies when they saw the box that Pingu was carrying, and they all rushed over to start eating it.

Then Pingu decided to go to the sad, old organ-grinder's house. He was sitting in his armchair looking very miserable when Pingu arrived.

"Have some popcorn," said Pingu cheerfully.

"How nice," said the organ-grinder. "I haven't had popcorn since I was a boy."

After that Pingu had one box of popcorn left.
"The baby McGreedy penguins seemed to like it,"
he thought to himself. "I'll see if they want some
more."

But Mrs McGreedy certainly did *not* want any more. Her baby penguins all had terrible tummy-ache from eating so much and there was popcorn just about everywhere.

"Would you like any more popcorn?" Pingu asked the postman.

But the postman didn't reply. He just groaned and shook his head.

Then Pinga had an idea.

"Let's pack the popcorn up in one of these crates," she said, "and post it off to someone."

"The organ-grinder seemed to be pleased with it," said Pingu, "so we could send him some more."

Pingu poured the popcorn into a crate and then he nailed the lid down securely with a hammer.

On the lid he wrote the name and address of the organ-grinder and then, when he had stuck the stamps on, the parcel was ready to go.

The postman took the parcel through his hatch and then set off on his sledge to deliver it.

The organ-grinder was sitting eating popcorn when the postman knocked on the door.

"Parcel for you," said the postman and put the crate down on the floor.

"Makes a change," said the organ-grinder. "I don't often get many parcels these days."

Suddenly the crate began to shudder and shake and then with a huge bang it burst open. Out came all the popcorn!

"Oh no!" groaned the organ-grinder, banging his fists on the table. "I can't face any more!"

24

Back at home Pingu and Pinga were gobbling up the rest of the popcorn as fast as they could. They had to get rid of it before Mum and Dad came home.

And at that moment, not far away, Mum and Dad were saying good-bye to their friends.

"Thank you for a lovely day," they said.

"Come again soon," said their friends.

"Quick, Pinga! Eat some more," said Pingu desperately. "Mum and Dad will be back any minute now."

When Mum and Dad came into the house a little later, all was quiet.

"Pingu and Pinga must be fast asleep," smiled Mum.

"I expect they'll wake up when they see what we've brought them," said Dad.

Mum came over and lifted the cover on the bed. Underneath she found Pingu and Pinga lying there with tummies blown up like balloons.

"Hullo," said Mum. "We've come home!"

Pingu and Pinga sat up with a jolt.

"We've brought you a special treat," said Mum. "Can you guess what it is?"

From behind their backs Mum and Dad produced two bags stuffed full of . . . popcorn!

Pingu and Pinga took one look at it and dived back under the bedclothes. Mum and Dad looked at each other in surprise.

"Maybe they only like homemade popcorn," said Mum. "I'll make some more in the morning!"

other PINGU books available from BBC Children's Books:

Pingu and his Family
Pingu and his Friends
Pingu and the Birthday Present
Pingu and the Kite
Pingu and the Seal
Pingu Has a Hard Time
Pingu Has Fun
Pingu in Trouble
Pingu the Adventurer
Pingu the Sportsman
Pingu the Star

Pingu the Postman Wheelie Book
Pingu Lift-the-Flap Book

Fun with Pingu Activity Book
Fun with Pingu Colouring Book

Pingu Chunky Books
Pingu and his Family
Pingu and his Grandpa
Pingu and the Seal
Pingu and his Sister

Published by BBC Children's Books
a division of BBC Enterprises Limited
Woodlands, 80 Wood Lane, London W12 0TT
First published 1994
Text © 1994 BBC Children's Books
Stills © 1994 Editoy/SRG/BBC Enterprises
Design © 1994 BBC Children's Books
Pingu © 1994 Editoy/SRG/BBC Enterprises

ISBN 0 563 40350 0

Typeset by BBC Children's Books
Colour separations by DOT Gradations, Chelmsford
Printed and bound by Cambus Litho, East Kilbride